THIS BOOK BELONGS TO:

_____

For Emma, Elsie and Emile and all bursting bears everywhere. M.R.

This paperback first published in 2013 by Andersen Press Ltd.
First published in Great Britain in 2012 by Andersen Press Ltd.,
20 Vauxhall Bridge Road, London SW1V 2SA.
Published in Australia by Random House Australia Pty.,
Level 3, 100 Pacific Highway, North Sydney, NSW 2060.
Text copyright © Michael Rosen, 2012
Illustrations copyright © Tony Ross, 2012
The rights of Michael Rosen and Tony Ross to be identified
as the author and illustrator of this work have been asserted
by them in accordance with the
Copyright, Designs and Patents Act, 1988.
All rights reserved.
Colour separated in Switzerland by Photolitho AG, Zürich.
Printed and bound in Singapore by Tien Wah Press.
Tony Ross has used pen, ink and watercolour in this book.

10   9   8   7   6   5   4   3   2   1

British Library Cataloguing in Publication Data available.
ISBN 978 1 84939 687 5

Bob the BURSTING Bear

MICHAEL ROSEN   TONY ROSS

ANDERSEN PRESS

It was lesson time at Toy School for Bob
and the other new toys.

"When you leave here, you are going to be looked
after by a boy or a girl," Mr Ted said.

The new toys were excited.

"But you will have to do special things to make sure that the boy or the girl cares for you and loves you," Mr Ted added.

"You must be fit," he said.

Mr Ted got all the toys to do exercises.

"You have to be clever," he said.

Mr Ted got all the toys to read books.

"And you have to be cuddly," he said.

Mr Ted showed all the toys how to be cuddly.

When they had all done this, Mr Ted looked at them proudly and said, "Now go out there and be loved!"

Bob the Bear packed his case and set off for his new home.

His new owner was called Solo.

When he arrived at her home, he was ready to be loved. He was fit, he was clever and he was cuddly.

But Solo's house was noisy. There were a lot
of people, and there was a lot going on.

In fact to tell the truth no one really noticed Bob the Bear.

Bob tried all sorts of things.

He did his exercises.

He read
some books.

He tried to look cuddly.

It was no good. That didn't work.
So, he tried some other things.

First, he tried making a noise . . .

but that didn't work.
There was a lot of noise going on already.

He tried falling over . . .

but that didn't work.
Everyone was always
falling over anyway.

He tried falling
off high places . . .

but that didn't work either.
All sorts of things fell
off high places in
Solo's house.

The next thing he tried was hiding.

But that didn't work. Wherever Bob hid, there were other things that were hiding or had got lost or had just disappeared from view ages ago.

So Bob tried something
completely different.

He remembered something he had read
in one of the books at Toy School.

He started to make himself
bigger . . .

bigger, and **bigger** and
bigger . . .

bigger

and **bigger** ...

Until he . . .

BURST with an enormous **BANG!**

Everyone stopped and looked.

Then they
started laughing.
They laughed
and laughed and
laughed.

"What a **BANG!**"
said Solo.
"It was amazing!"
said Solo's brother.
"It's Bob the
Bursting Bear!"
said Solo's cousin.

They collected up all the bits of Bob
that were lying around . . .

this bit here, that bit there, this bit on that bit . . .

until at last Bob was put back together.
Not exactly, exactly the same as he was before . . .

but more or less.

"Again!" shouted Solo.

So Bob the Bear started
to make himself

bigger …

bigger, and **bigger** …

bigger ...

and **bigger** ...

All over again
until he ...

BURST with an enormous **BANG!**

"Hooray!" everyone shouted.
"Bob the Bursting Bear!" they shouted.

Now everyone wanted Bob the Bear.
Now everyone loved Bob – Bob the Bursting Bear!

Other books to enjoy:

9781842704929

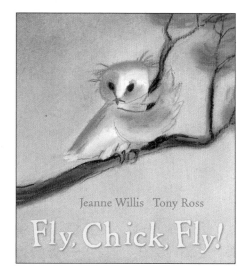

9781849394383

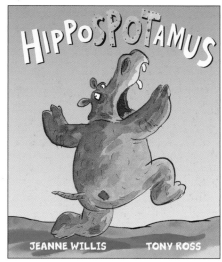

9781849394161

9781842704264

9781849393195

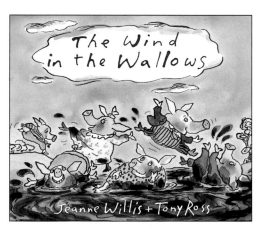

9781849394536